*To R.V.A., my Mom,
who instilled in me a love of reading
—J.A.G.*

*For Anne
—S.T.*

I Can Read!™

SHARED
My
First
READING

Chicken Said, "Cluck!"

by Judyann Ackerman Grant
pictures by Sue Truesdell

HARPER

An Imprint of HarperCollinsPublishers

Chicken Said, "Cluck!" Text copyright © 2008 by Judyann Ackerman Grant Illustrations copyright © 2008 by Sue Truesdell All rights reserved. Manufactured in China. No part of this book may be used or reproduced in any manner whatsoever without written permission except in the case of brief quotations embodied in critical articles and reviews. For information address HarperCollins Children's Books, a division of HarperCollins Publishers, 195 Broadway, New York, NY 10007.
www.icanread.com

Library of Congress Cataloging-in-Publication Data

Grant, Judyann Ackerman

Chicken said, "cluck!" / by Judyann Ackerman Grant ; pictures by Sue Truesdell.—1st ed.

p.   cm.(An I can read book)

Summary: Earl and Pearl do not want Chicken's help in the garden, until a swarm of grasshoppers arrives and her true talent shines.

ISBN 978-0-06-028723-8 (trade bdg.) — ISBN 978-0-06-444276-3 (pbk.)

[1. Chickens—Fiction. 2. Gardening—Fiction. 3. Grasshoppers—Fiction.] I. Grant, Judyann Ackerman. II. Title. III. Series.

PZ7.G766775Ch 2008

[E] 21

2001024016

CIP

AC

17 18 19 20   SCP   15 14 13 12 11   ❖   First Edition

"I will grow a pumpkin,"
said Earl.

"I will grow two pumpkins,"
said Pearl.
Chicken scratched the dirt.

"Shoo!" said Earl.

"Shoo! Shoo!" said Pearl.

"Cluck! Cluck! Cluck!"
said Chicken.

Earl dug the garden.

Pearl planted the seeds.

Chicken scratched the dirt.
"Shoo!" said Earl.

"Shoo! Shoo!" said Pearl.

"Cluck! Cluck! Cluck!"
said Chicken.

Earl watered the seeds.

Pearl pulled the weeds.

Chicken scratched the dirt.

"Shoo!" said Earl.

"Shoo! Shoo!" said Pearl.

"Cluck! Cluck! Cluck!"

said Chicken.

Earl's pumpkin grew.

Pearl's pumpkins grew.

Chicken scratched the dirt.

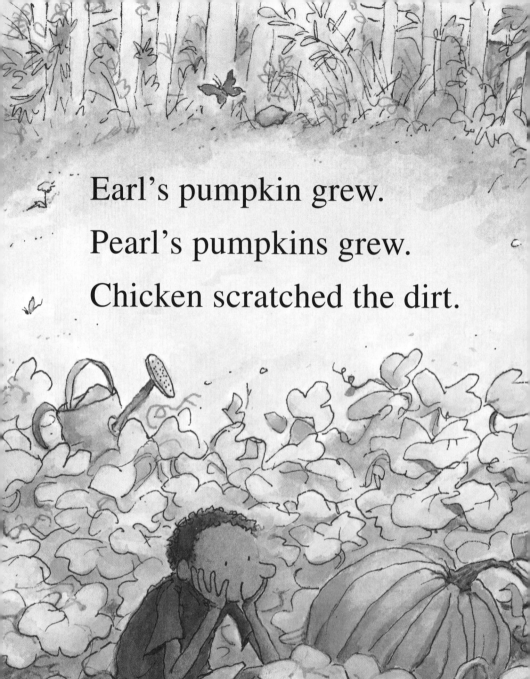

"Shoo!" said Earl.

"Shoo! Shoo!" said Pearl.

"Cluck! Cluck! Cluck!"
said Chicken.

Then one day
grasshoppers came.

Jump! In the garden.

Nibble.

Jump! On the pumpkins.

Nibble. Nibble.

Jump! Jump! Jump!

Nibble. Nibble. Nibble.

"Shoo!" said Earl.

"Shoo! Shoo!" said Pearl.

The grasshoppers stayed.

Chicken said, "Cluck!"

One grasshopper jumped.

Chicken said,
"Cluck! Cluck!"
Two grasshoppers jumped.

Chicken said,
"Cluck! Cluck! Cluck!"
Jump! Jump! Jump!

27

"Hooray!" said Earl.

"Hooray! Hooray!" said Pearl.

"Cluck! Cluck! Cluck!"
said Chicken.

Earl gave Chicken
one pumpkin.

Pearl gave Chicken
two pumpkins.

Chicken scratched the dirt.